Copyright year 2011
Copyright notice By Nick Carter.
All rights reserved.
The above information forms this copyright notice
2011 by Nick Carter.
All Illustrations Copyright © 2011 Nathan Stell

This book belongs to

_____

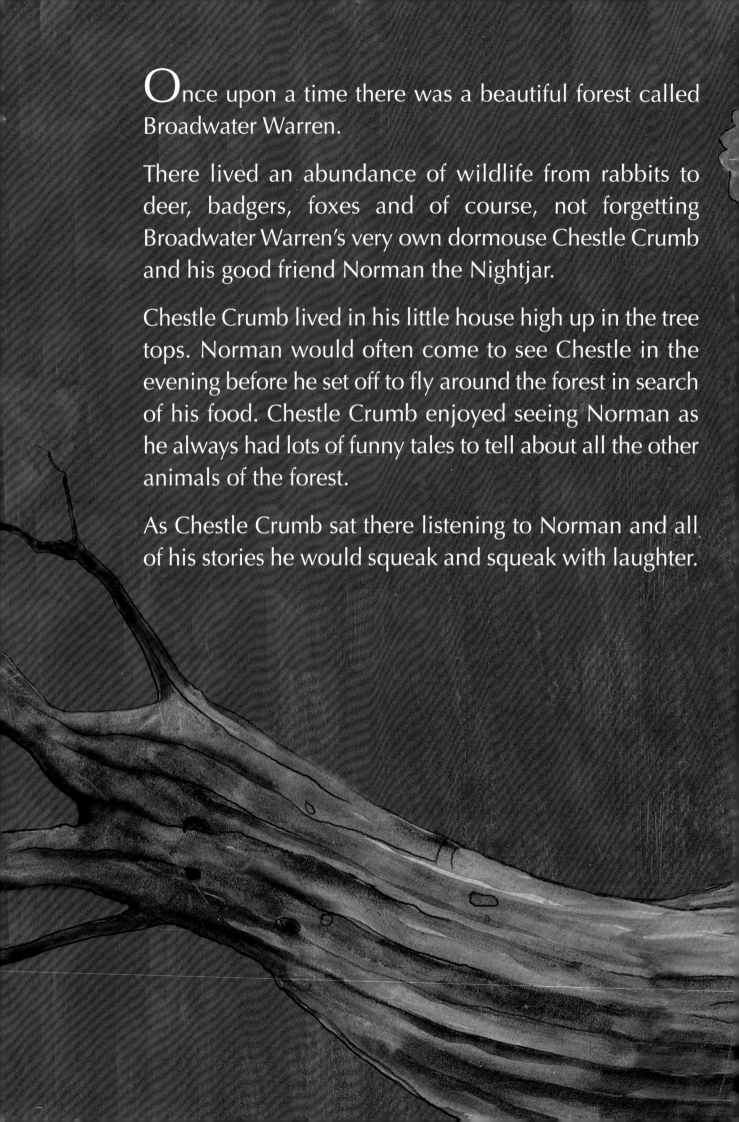

Once upon a time there was a beautiful forest called Broadwater Warren.

There lived an abundance of wildlife from rabbits to deer, badgers, foxes and of course, not forgetting Broadwater Warren's very own dormouse Chestle Crumb and his good friend Norman the Nightjar.

Chestle Crumb lived in his little house high up in the tree tops. Norman would often come to see Chestle in the evening before he set off to fly around the forest in search of his food. Chestle Crumb enjoyed seeing Norman as he always had lots of funny tales to tell about all the other animals of the forest.

As Chestle Crumb sat there listening to Norman and all of his stories he would squeak and squeak with laughter.

Norman told him about the night when Billy the badger put his nose into an ants nest and when he came out he looked like Rudolf the red-nosed reindeer after being bitten by all the ants.

"Poor old Billy," Chestle squeaked. "He always seems to get himself into some kind of trouble."

"That he does!" Norman chirred. "By the way, I have some very good news for you Chestle. Mistle the deer has given birth to a beautiful fawn. She has named her Sandy as she was born beside the Sand Rock on the far side of the forest."

Chestle was so delighted and said he would arrange a special party with all the other animals to welcome Mistle's newborn baby into the forest.

"Oh Chestle, What a wonderful idea" Norman squawked. "Would you like me to find the perfect place for the party? I can do that tonight while I am out flying."

"Ok" Chestle squeaked, "Off you go then, we have a lot to do. I will spread the word around to all the other animals of the forest." Chestle set off towards the decoy pond as he knew most of the animals would be there as they liked to drink water at night.

As he got closer to the pond he could hear lots of splashing around and a funny sort of barking noise. It was Freda the fox she was by the side of the decoy pond watching her cubs playing.

They were chasing each other in and around the reed beds and jumping around in the water.

"Freda" Chestle called "I need your help. We are going to arrange a party for Mistle, to welcome her newborn baby into the forest."

Freda thought this was a marvellous idea and asked if there was anything she could do to help out. Chestle knew Freda was very good at making things and asked if she would be kind enough to make a special present for Mistle the deer's baby fawn.

"Oh yes of course I will." Freda barked. "How about a nice bed for her baby? We could gather up some of the fern from the forest, it will be nice and comfortable for her to sleep on at night."

"That's very kind of you." Chestle squeaked. "I am sure Mistle's baby would love that." With that, Freda and her cubs ran into the forest in search of lots of dry fern.

As Chestle set off on his journey to his little house in the tree Norman the Nightjar flew overhead and landed just in front of him.

"I found it, I found it!" he chirred. "The perfect place for the party."

Chestle put his tiny paws around Norman's beak.
"Not so loud Norman," he whispered. If Mistle is close by she might hear us, you know how good a deer's hearing can be.".

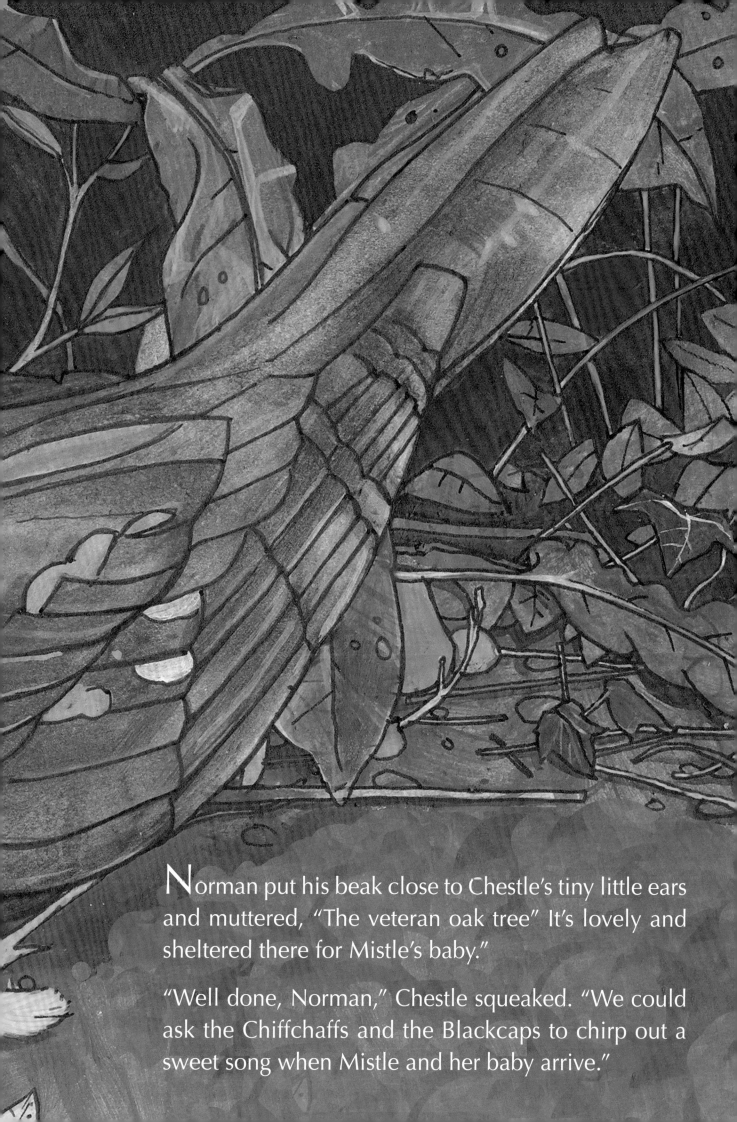

Norman put his beak close to Chestle's tiny little ears and muttered, "The veteran oak tree" It's lovely and sheltered there for Mistle's baby."

"Well done, Norman," Chestle squeaked. "We could ask the Chiffchaffs and the Blackcaps to chirp out a sweet song when Mistle and her baby arrive."

Meanwhile back in the forest, Freda the fox and her cubs were busy making Sandy's new bed. Her cubs had been running to and fro collecting lots of fern for her to make the bed with. The cubs loved doing this as they could chase each other around the forest and get up to lots of mischief while their mother was not watching them.

Freda the fox barked loudly to let the cubs know that she had finished making Sandy's new bed and that it was now time for them to go home to their den.

Their father had been out searching for their supper while they had been busy making Sandy's present.

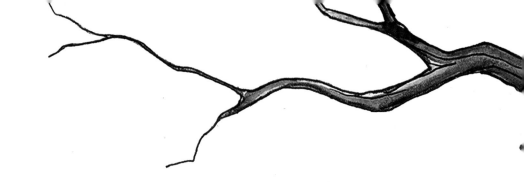

Chestle Crumb and Norman the Nightjar were sitting up in the tree talking about Mistle the deer's surprise party, When suddenly they heard the marching of thousand's of tiny feet.

"Hello?" came a voice from below Chestle's house. "We hear there is going to be a party to welcome Mistle's newborn baby and you need our help."

It was Worton the wood ant and his mighty army. Worton and his army of ants were very small, but altogether in their thousands, they could build anything. They had a very nasty bite, as Billy the badger found out earlier after poking his nose into their nest.

Chestle explained to Worton that they needed somewhere for all the animals to sit down and something that was comfortable for all the animals of the forest.

"Oh that's easy." Worton replied. "You leave that to us, we will climb the oak trees and get lots and lots of leaves, I am sure they will be very comfortable to sit on."

With that, Worton and his army of ants went back down the tree singing their favourite song.

"We are the wood ants and we are small,

Together we are strong and we beat all,

We wander these woods and we never rest,

Do not put your nose in our ants nest".

Meanwhile back in Valley Mire Mistle the deer was grazing in the forest when all of a sudden she heard the sound of rustling from inside of the ferns.

Mistle called out to Sandy as she was not sure whether Sandy was in danger, when out from the ferns appeared Billy the badger. "Sorry to startle you," Billy grunted, "Chestle has asked to see you."

"Whatever for?" Mistle replied.
"I don't know," Billy grunted. "Are you coming or not? I have not got all day, you know!"

With that Billy scuffled around and headed off into the depth of the ferns. Mistle nudged Sandy and she got up onto her rather unsteady legs and they both set off.

"This way," Billy grunted as he headed off into the forest. It was a good job Billy had white on his fur as it was very dark. Poor Mistle had trouble keeping up as Sandy was still weak and unsteady on her feet. Mistle had no idea where Billy was taking her. He certainly was not heading towards Chestle's home.

Mistle and Sandy were sure in for a big surprise as all the other animals of the forest had gathered by the veteran oak tree for their party.

Norman had been sitting up high on the tree tops at the end of the woodland path.

Chestle had asked him to keep lookout for Mistle and Sandy and when they were close by to let him know, so that all the animals of the forest could hide for their surprise party.

"She's coming! She's coming!" Norman chirred. Chestle gave the signal for all the animals to hide.

There was Worton and the wood ants hiding on the top of the tall oak tree leaves and Freda and her cubs hid in the newly dug hole in the ground.

The Chiffchaffs and the Blackcaps were on the top of the tree ready to chirp out their song and good old Norman the Nightjar was halfway up the tree next to Chestle trying his best to be very quiet.

As Mistle and her baby fawn got closer to the tree, Mistle lost sight of Billy the badger he just seemed to have vanished into thin air.

Mistle stood by the Veteran oak tree calling out for Chestle when all of a sudden all the animals of the forest came out from their hiding places and shouted out,

"Surprise!"

Poor Mistle had no idea what the surprise was for but she was very happy about it.

"Mistle," Chestle squeaked. "This party is for your newborn baby to welcome her into the forest. Freda and her cubs have made a present for Sandy.

With that, Freda's cubs gently picked up Sandy's present and dropped it down beside Mistle's feet. It was a beautiful bed just for Sandy. My, how she loved it! Sandy nestled down and went straight to sleep.

Mistle looked down at Sandy and a teardrop landed on top of Sandy's nose, all the animals laughed as it made Sandy sneeze out loud!

For the rest of the evening all the animals of the forest sat around sharing stories with one another, while up in the treetops the Chiffchaffs and the Blackcaps sang their sweet songs.

The End

I would like to thank the RSPB and the High Weald
for their help and advice throughout this story.

Thank you to
David Warren
Manor Business Solutions.
Victoria James Inns Ltd.

For their kind sponsorship of this new story.

Thank you to June Spencer for all your help
throughout my writing of this new book.

This book is for you mum

Printed by Wealden Print, Hawkhurst, 2017